Dear Parent:
Your child's love of reading starts here!

Every child learns to read in a different way and at his or her own speed. Some go back and forth between reading levels and read favorite books again and again. Others read through each level in order. You can help your young reader improve and become more confident by encouraging his or her own interests and abilities. From books your child reads with you to the first books he or she reads alone, there are I Can Read Books for every stage of reading:

SHARED READING
Basic language, word repetition, and whimsical illustrations, ideal for sharing with your emergent reader

BEGINNING READING
Short sentences, familiar words, and simple concepts for children eager to read on their own

READING WITH HELP
Engaging stories, longer sentences, and language play for developing readers

READING ALONE
Complex plots, challenging vocabulary, and high-interest topics for the independent reader

ADVANCED READING
Short paragraphs, chapters, and exciting themes for the perfect bridge to chapter books

I Can Read Books have introduced children to the joy of reading since 1957. Featuring award-winning authors and illustrators and a fabulous cast of beloved characters, I Can Read Books set the standard for beginning readers.

A lifetime of discovery begins with the magical words **"I Can Read!"**

Visit www.icanread.com for information
on enriching your child's reading experience.

I Can Read!™ SHARED My First READING

JUST A
LITTLE LOVE

BY MERCER MAYER

HARPER
An Imprint of HarperCollins*Publishers*

*For the children, teachers, and families of Sandy Hook,
with all my love.*

I Can Read Book® is a trademark of HarperCollins Publishers.

Little Critter: Just a Little Love

Library of Congress card number: 2013938122
ISBN 978-0-06-207196-5 (trade bdg.)—ISBN 978-0-06-147815-4 (pbk.)
13 14 15 16 17   LP/WOR   10 9 8 7 6 5 4 3 2
❖
First Edition

A Big Tuna Trading Company, LLC/J.R. Sansevere Book
www.littlecritter.com

Grandpa calls and says
Grandma isn't feeling very well.

We decide to go and
cheer her up with love.

I draw a get well card
just for Grandma.
Little Sister helps.

Mom makes egg salad.

She puts olives in it.

I love olives, but I spill them.

"Look, Mom," I say.

"Blue loves olives, too!"

Little Sister picks flowers
just for Grandma.

But a bee stings her.
Mom gives her a little love.
Then she feels better.

We pick apples for Grandma.
We put them in a basket.
I fall off the ladder.

I do not cry much.

Dad gives me some love.

I feel better.

I carry the apples to the car.

I do not see Blue.

I step on Blue's tail.

Blue says, "Yelp!"

Now Blue needs a little love.

Blue feels better.

Little Sister brings her dolls
to show Grandma.
Mom says, "No, take two."

Little Sister says,

"My other dolls are lonely.

They need lots of love."

Kitty finds the egg salad.
Oh, no! Blue finds it, too!

We have no egg salad.

Mom is sad.

She needs a little love.

It is time to leave.

I say good-bye to my pets.

They look sad. I hug them.

I see a turtle in the road.
"Dad!" I say. "Save the turtle.
Turtles need love, too."

Dad picks up the turtle.

Dad puts him in the grass.

He is safe. We wave good-bye.

I need to use the bathroom.

Dad stops at a gas station.

I flush the toilet.

The water pours everywhere.

I say thank you and leave.

A man on a motorcycle
with flashing lights
tells Dad to pull over.

He is a state trooper.

He gives Dad a ticket,

but not for a ball game.

Dad does not look too happy.

We all give Dad some love.

Now he will feel better.

Dad starts the car.

We have a nice slow drive

all the rest of the way.

Here we are.

Grandma is not in bed.

She is sitting with Grandpa.

I say, "Grandma, I thought you weren't feeling well."
Grandma says, "I wasn't.

"I just needed a little love."
I say, "Me, too, Grandma!"